About the Author

Margaret grew up in the North East of Scotland and studied Sports Development and Health Promotion at University. She spent 9 Summers at Camp Blue Ridge, which is a Summer Camp based in Northern Georgia in the USA, as a Camp Counsellor, Unit Leader and Sports Director. She also spent 7 years in Eastern North Carolina, working at YMCA Camp Sea Gull/Camp Seafarer as an Operations/Program Assistant which is where she and Jimmy, the Dalmatian, first met up until their return to Scotland in 2015 to help care for her terminally ill Mother which became the beginning of her journey as a Children's Author following Jimmy's actual life events.

Margaret Scott

Jimmy Gets a Pet Passport

AUSTIN MACAULEY PUBLISHERS™

LONDON • CAMBRIDGE • NEW YORK • SHARJAH

A CIP catalogue record for this title is available from the British Library.

ISBN 9781788485722 (Paperback)
ISBN 9781788485739 (Hardback)
ISBN 9781788485746 (E-Book)
www.austinmacauley.com

First Published (2018)
Austin Macauley Publishers ™ Ltd
25 Canada Square
Canary Wharf
London
E14 5LQ

Dedication

Highland Hospice is a registered Scottish Charity - Charity No SCO11227 and will receive £1 from each book sale.

James, Margaret and the Highland Hospice

Jimmy is a 3-year old lovable, energetic Dalmatian who loves to go on adventures. She is a special dog, because she always tries her best to be gentle and kind.

Jimmy was born in America with lots of brothers and sisters and when she was 8 weeks old, she and her sister went to live in North Carolina. Jimmy's new Mummy was born in Scotland and moved to America to help take care of children and families at a Summer Camp.

Jimmy loved life at Camp Seafarer, which was the Summer Camp, where her new Mummy lived. She spent most of her days running and playing with her other spotted friends in the warm sunshine. This was one of Jimmy's favourite things to do.

One day, Jimmy's Mummy picked her up from the playpen and held her very tightly. "Jimmy, we are going on an adventure to meet your Scottish Family," said Jimmy's Mummy, wondering if Jimmy would like that.

Jimmy jumped up and out of her Mummy's arms with excitement. She started running around in circles as fast as she could and then suddenly, she stopped.

What will my family look like? she thought. *Will my family like me?* she wondered. *Will my family have spots like me?* she asked herself.

The next day, Jimmy woke up. She yawned and stretched and wriggled her way out from under the covers. Jimmy loved sleeping in a big bed with lots of blankets. "Wakey-wakey," said Jimmy's Mummy." It's time to go to the Vet for your check-up." Jimmy did not like going to the Vet. Jimmy had taken lots of trips to the Vet and sometimes the Vet would give her medicine that tasted SO bad.

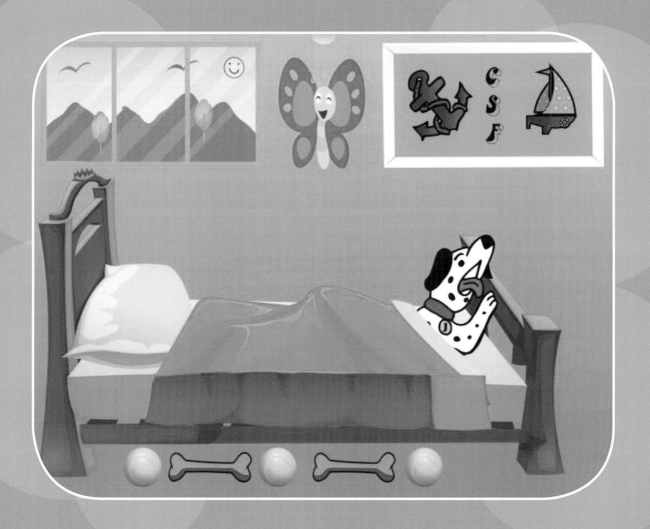

"OK, let's go," said Jimmy's Mummy as she opened the car door for Jimmy to jump inside. "Just think once you have your check-up, you will have a Pet Passport, and that means you can go on an aeroplane."

Jimmy jumped into the car and started to remember her last trip to the Vet. She was not all that fond of the Vet. She did not like getting injections. Going to the Vet was one of her least favourite things to do. Sometimes she slept there, and Jimmy did not like being away from her Mummy.

They walked into the Animal Hospital, and Jimmy tried to hide behind a chair, hoping that no one could see her. Very soon, the Vet called her name. "It's OK, Jimmy, remember the Vet helps you stay healthy, everything will be OK, trust me," said Jimmy's Mummy, leading her into a small room with a big table.

The Vet was a lady who Jimmy had seen before. "How can we help you today?" said the Vet as she walked towards Jimmy. "Jimmy needs to get a check-up so that she can get a Pet Passport, because we are moving to Scotland," said Jimmy's Mummy as she tried to stop Jimmy from hiding behind her legs.

"OK, let's get started," said the Vet. "We need to check her weight, give her some medicine to make sure that she does not have any bugs in her tummy and then make sure her injections are up to date."

Jimmy did what she was told and followed the Vet. She took her medicine at the first time of asking even though, it tasted SO bad. *Yuck*, she thought as she tried to swallow it as fast as she could.

"Here you go," said the Vet, who handed Jimmy's mummy a large piece of paper. "Jimmy will need to travel with this so that she can be checked onto the aeroplane and then again in London at the Animal Reception Centre." The Vet bent down to give Jimmy a pat. "You will be OK, Jimmy," she whispered. "I promise everything will be OK."

Jimmy raced out of the Vet, dragging her Mummy behind her. "Slow down, Jimmy!" said Jimmy's Mummy as Jimmy slowed down just in time to jump into her car. "Our next adventure is going to be sleeping in a dog-friendly hotel," said Jimmy's Mummy as she grabbed the car door to stop herself from falling over.

Jimmy settled down, in the front seat of her car, happy that the Vet's trip was now over. Her Mummy reached in to fasten her seatbelt and gave her an ear rub. Jimmy loved getting her ears rubbed. It always made her feel safe and sleepy.

Her eyes closed after a quick look to make sure her Mummy was still there. *A Hotel?* thought Jimmy, finding herself puzzled once again. As long as Jimmy was with her Mummy, she knew, everything would be OK.